BERNARD WABER

EVIE & MARGIE

Houghton Mifflin Company Boston 2003
Walter Lorraine Books

For Amanda, Cameron, Matthew, Zachary, Tyler, Sarah, Daniel — and for Eve Feldman

Walter Lorraine
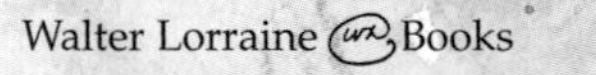
Books

www.houghtonmifflinbooks.com

Library of Congress Cataloging-in-Publication Data

Waber, Bernard.
Evie and Margie / Bernard Waber.
p. cm.
"Walter Lorraine Books."
Summary: Best friends, Evie and Margie the hippopotamuses, are surprised to experience jealousy when they try out for the same part in the school play.
ISBN 0-618-34124-2
[1. Friendship—Fiction. 2. Jealousy—Fiction. 3. Theater—Fiction. 4. Actors and actresses—Fiction. 5. Schools—Fiction. 6. Hippopotamus—Fiction.] I. Title.
PZ7.W113Ev 2003
[E]—dc21

2003000533

Printed in the United States of América
WOZ 10 9 8 7 6 5 4 3 2 1

Evie and Margie were best friends.
They did everything together.

They even dreamed together.
They dreamed of becoming actors.
"Someday we'll be famous," said Evie.
"Someday everyone will want
our autographs," said Margie.
"We'll change our names," said Evie.
"Mine will be Mariah," said Margie.
"Mine will be Eliza," said Evie.

"And we'll always be best friends,"
they promised each other.

STARRING
ELIZA
STARRING
MARIAH

But then something happened to test their friendship.
It began when Mr. Stanniss, their teacher, announced:
"I am happy to tell you that our class was selected to present this year's play. We'll be doing *Cinderella,* and next week everyone can try out for parts."

Evie and Margie both decided to try out for the lead role, the part of Cinderella.
"But deep down I'll want you to get it," said Margie.
"And deep down I'll want you," said Evie.

They began at once to practice for the tryouts.

"Let's work on the part where Cinderella cries when she can't go to the ball," said Margie. "Crying parts are so *grrreat*. You first."

"All right," said Evie, making a crying face. "Boo-hoo, I want to go to the ball, too."

"How was that?" said Evie.

"Ummm . . . okay," said Margie.

"Just . . . okay?"

"You could have cried with real tears," said Margie.

"Real tears?" said Evie.

“Watch me,”said Margie.

“Boo-hoo,” Margie began in a faint, weepy voice,

“I want to go to the ball, too.”

Suddenly, Margie’s eyes filled with tears.

Real tears. Gigantic tears.

Tears that quickly became enormous puddles

spilling and splashing down her cheeks.

And then, just as suddenly . . .

she moaned . . .

shook . . .

swooned . . .

and fell, sobbing, on the bed.

"Margie! Margie! Are you all right?"

Evie cried out to her.

Margie giggled.
"Of course I'm all right.
I was acting."

"Wow," said Evie. "How did you do that?"
"Easy," said Margie. "I just remembered something bad that happened to me—something really, really bad.
Something so bad, and so sad, just thinking about it made me cry. My cousin Harriet taught me how to do that.
She took acting classes at summer camp, you know."

"What bad thing happened?" said Evie.

"It's a secret," said Margie.

"A secret from me?" said Evie.

"Even from you," said Margie. "It has to be a secret. Harriet warned me about that. Keeping it secret is the magic—the magic for crying real tears."

"Now you try it," said Margie.

"But nothing bad ever happened to me," said Evie.

"Pretend, then," said Margie. "Pretend something bad happened to you—or someone you care about."

"Oh, no," said Evie.

"It's only pretend," said Margie.

Evie looked at the clock.
"I have to go home,"
she said.

That night, just before bedtime, Evie tried to think of something bad or sad that had happened to her. Little by little something came to her.

She remembered a kindergarten birthday party, and how she cried and cried because they ran out of cupcakes just when it was her turn to take one—her favorite kind, too, with pink and purple sprinkles.

And then she remembered crying even harder when she was offered a carrot stick instead.

"Perfect," thought Evie. "I'll use that."
So Evie squeezed her eyes real tight, and with all her might tried to feel again the sting of missing out on that long-ago, most-yearned-for cupcake.

Evie got all set for tears, but no tears came. She squeezed her eyes again and again. She squeezed and squeezed and squeezed until her face turned purple from squeezing.
Still no tears.

Now Evie was exasperated. Now Evie was *really* exasperated. Now Evie was so exasperated, she finally forced herself to take Margie's advice. She pretended something bad happened to her parents.

Evie was so frightened by what she pretended,
she ran to her parents and hugged them
and kissed them a dozen times.
"Evie is such a tender child," said her mother.
"She most certainly is," said her father.

That night Evie slept
with her parents.

The next night Evie tried again. This time she pretended
something terrible happened to her dog, Morris.
She pretended Morris was lost

Pretending Morris was lost shook Evie up so much, she ran to Morris and hugged him and patted him and kissed him, too, a dozen times.

That night Evie slept with Morris.

The next night Evie tried again. This time she pretended
something awful happened to her pet fish, Goldie.
She pretended that Goldie, in a moment of gleeful friskiness,
leaped from her bowl and lay huffing and puffing
on the coffee table.

Picturing Goldie so helpless tore Evie apart.
She ran to Goldie, hugged her fishbowl,
and kissed it, too, a dozen times.

That night
Evie slept
with Goldie.

Next it was Evie's turn.
Evie decided to give
her sad cupcake memory
a second chance.
She blinked hard to coax tears,
but all she got was one measly tear
that somehow was lost trickling
down her cheek.
"Nice, Evie," said Mr. Stanniss.

Tryouts were held the next day.
Margie was first.
Everyone was astonished
by her free-flowing tears.
Mr. Stanniss even ran for tissues
and helped dry her eyes.
"That was so moving, Margie,"
he said.

"Now here's what we'll do," Mr. Stanniss went on.
"Margie will play Cinderella, and Evie will be her understudy.
That means if Margie can't perform in the play,
Evie will take her place. Evie will be Cinderella."

"Does it also mean I won't be in the play?"
said Evie.
"You'll have enough to do learning Cinderella's lines,"
said Mr. Stanniss. "So in the play you can be a tree
in the forest. As Cinderella runs past,
you will say, '*Whoosh!*'"

Evie tried hard to feel happy for Margie, but at home she cried and cried. Real tears. Honest tears. Big sloppy tears—bigger, fatter, and wetter tears than Margie's. And bit by bit, sob by sob, gulp by gulp, sniffle by sniffle, she blurted out what had happened—how she ended up playing a tree, and how her only line in the entire play was *whoosh!*

"*Whoosh?*" said her mother.

"*Whoosh?*" said her father.

"Yes, *whoosh,*" cried Evie. "And I don't even feel like a tree," she burst out, with fresh tears.

Her father dried Evie's eyes and let her blow her nose into his handkerchief. And then he said,

"Listen, Evie, you're going to go out there and slam that word *whoosh* right out of the ballpark. You're going to be the best *whoosher* you can possibly be. You're going to *whoosh* like nobody has ever *whooshed.* Do you hear me, Evie? *Slugger?"*

"I hear you," sobbed Evie, "but I still hate, hate, hate my part."

So every night Evie practiced her one lonely line.

"*Whoosh! Whoosh!*" she said in different ways.

"*Whoosh! Whoosh!*" she said in different voices, with different gestures. "*Whoosh! Whoosh! Whoosh!*"

And every day she rehearsed the Cinderella role with Margie.

At last the big day arrived—the day of the show.
That morning Evie awoke feeling that something was
wrong. Something just didn't feel right.

Soon she knew what was wrong
and what didn't feel right.
She was jealous of Margie.

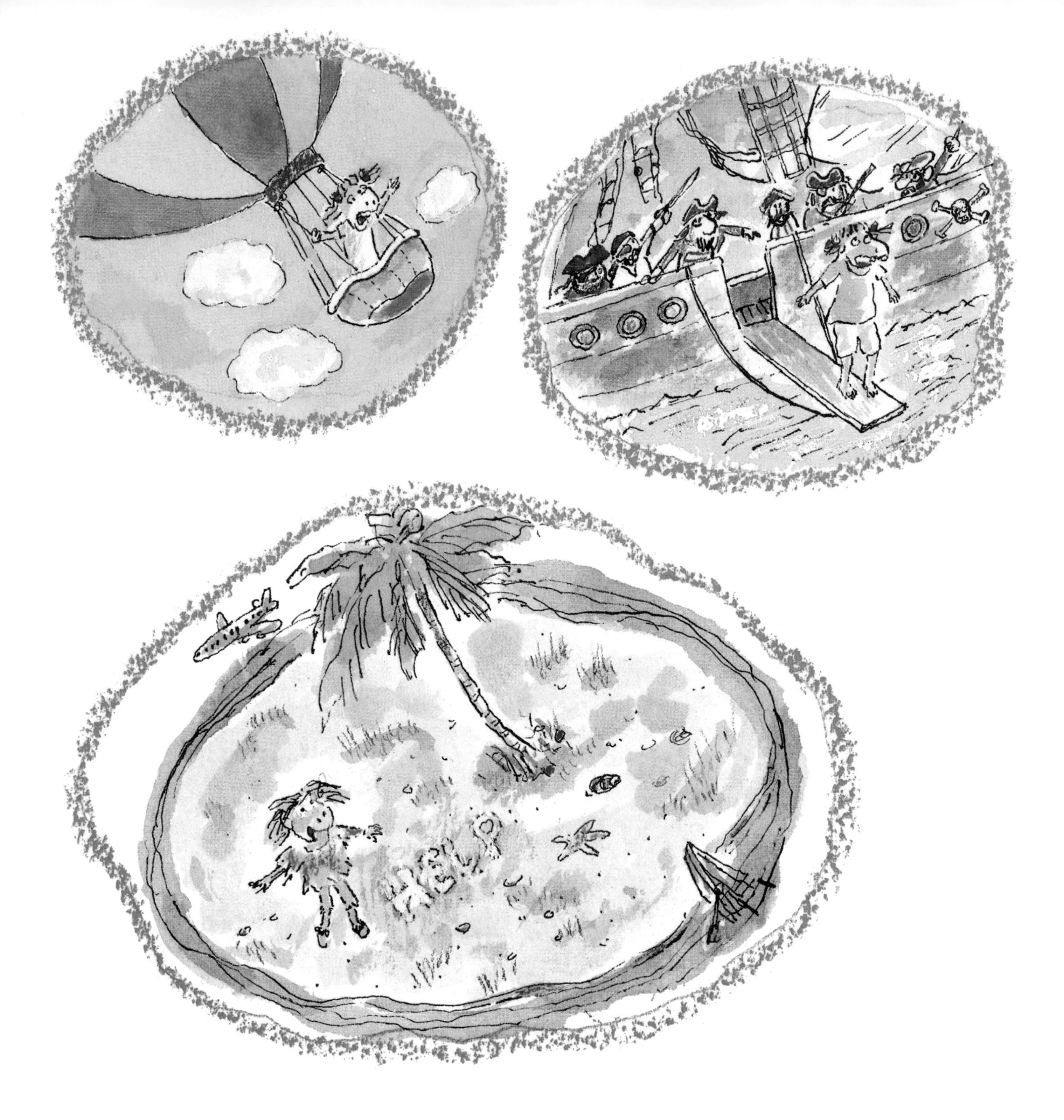

Even worse, and much against her will, she began to imagine all manner of circumstances that would prevent Margie from performing in the play.

Evie was so terrified by her jealousy, she welcomed the ringing of the telephone. It was Margie.

"Guess what?" Margie sobbed. "I can't be in the play.
I have the worst cold."

"Oh, no," said Evie. "I feel so bad for you." And Evie meant it. She knew, too painfully, how rotten it felt to be disappointed.

"Good luck playing Cinderella," Margie cried as she hung up.

Evie arrived at school in a daze.
"Quickly," said an anxious Mr. Stanniss, "get into the Cinderella costume."

Soon after, the curtain parted and Evie stepped unsteadily onto the stage. She quickly got hold of herself, and when it was time for the big crying scene, Evie was ready.
She cried real tears remembering her bitter disappointment with the tree part. And she cried many more tears for Margie's disappointment. But she cried the most tears because being jealous felt so horrible.

The audience cried with her.

Even Mr. Stanniss cried—possibly from relief.

When the play was over, everyone cheered for Evie.

After school, Evie immediately called Margie.

"I heard you were *grrreat,*" said Margie.

"But it should have been you playing Cinderella," said Evie.

"Oh, good news," said Margie. "Mr. Stanniss told my mom the play was so wonderful, they're planning another performance. And this time, when I am well, I will be Cinderella. Isn't that *grrreat!*"

"*Grrreat!*" said Evie. "And I'll gladly play the tree."

"*Whoosh!*" Margie said, kiddingly.

"Margie, I have something terrible to tell you," said Evie. "I was jealous of you, and I'm so ashamed."

Margie was quiet for a moment, and then she said, "I was jealous of you, too, Evie."

"You were? Oh, *grrreat!*" said Evie. "I feel so much better now."

"Gotta go," said Margie. "Luv yuh, Eliza."

"Luv yuh, Mariah," said Evie.

The following week Margie was well enough to play Cinderella. Everyone agreed she was wonderful in the role—especially Evie.

And after that they had an ice cream party to celebrate both performances. Oh, and guess what?

Evie had a cupcake with her ice cream.
And guess what else?
Her favorite kind—
with pink and purple sprinkles.